The TREASURE · HUNT

It was a cold, wet winter and the crew of the good ship *Barleycorn* was bored.

Now this was no ordinary crew, for all seven of its members were mice, and no ordinary mice either. For they were pirates, and they spent their lives sailing the high seas in search of adventure.

But on this day it seemed there were no adventures to be found. Instead, the Captain and his mousey men peered miserably through the windows of the old lighthouse where they lived and dreamed of other things. Of gorgonzola cheese and ship's biscuits, of warm sun and tropical islands far away, of sea monsters and stormy oceans, and – of course – of treasure…

Even Nelson, the ship's parrot, was dreaming of finding diamonds as big as peanuts when a shout from Horatio nearly knocked him off his perch. Now Horatio *never* stopped looking for adventure, and he usually found one around every corner.

Luckily, this day was no exception, for what do you think he had found under the floorboards of that old abandoned lighthouse? Why an old sea scroll, of course. And old and dusty though it was, there was no mistaking that on it there was a map…

H oratio ran to the Captain's table and unrolled the ancient scroll. His shipmates gathered round, all thoughts of gorgonzola gone as they stared at the curious scene before them.

For on one side of the map was a drawing of a strange ocean full of whirlpools and warnings of sea serpents and shipwrecks, and among them, a series of tiny islands beside which was written:

> *"Go sailing west towards the sun*
> *For seven days and you will come*
> *To this great ocean o'er the sea,*
> *Where seven islands wait for thee.*
> *On some are birds, or snakes, or cats.*
> *Another's overrun by rats.*
> *The fifth is made of pirates' bones,*
> *And echoes to their ghostly groans.*
> *A sixth has seashells without measure,*
> *But only one hides buried treasure."*

And sure enough, as the mice looked hard at the drawings, they saw the secret signs that told them which island was which.

"We must set sail at once!" cried the Captain. "All aboard for an adventure!"

Can you see which island holds the treasure?
Look carefully at the map and you will find it.

When they reached the island, they rowed
their boat up onto the sandy shore.
"And where to now?" said Horatio, puzzled.
"What does the next clue say?" asked Blighty, afraid
of what might be in store. So Horatio read:

"This clue will come out of the air –
The only one not in a pair.
A lonely wanderer comes to rest,
And leads you to the treasure chest."

All the mice looked up at the great blue sky, and as
they looked, it seemed to become full of birds.
"Aha!" cried the Captain triumphantly. "I know
what the clue means! Can't you see?"

**Can you help the mice
by finding the one bird that
does not have a partner?**

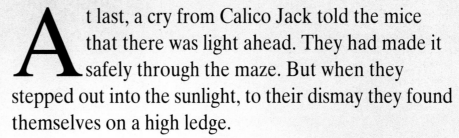

At last, a cry from Calico Jack told the mice that there was light ahead. They had made it safely through the maze. But when they stepped out into the sunlight, to their dismay they found themselves on a high ledge.

Before them stretched a great jungle valley full of huge trees. The branches of the nearest one grew right beside the ledge itself, and the mice could see brightly colored birds and dancing butterflies among its leaves.

Huge vines covered in beautiful flowers curled around the branches. And when Flagpole Jo (who had the best head for heights) looked over the edge of the ledge, he saw that some of the vines hung right down to the ground. And the map said:

"Pick a vine and down you climb.
But be careful: take your time.
Don't pick one that doesn't go
To the forest far below."

Can you see which vines will lead the mice to the forest floor?

S oon all the mice had clambered safely down the vines. The forest below was full of colorful insects – butterflies as big as dinner plates danced around their heads, and shiny beetles scuttled this way and that between their feet.

Paths led off through the forest in all directions. But which one should they follow?

"Perhaps the map will give us a clue," suggested Calico Jack. So Horatio read:

"Insects, insects all around,
In the air and on the ground.
If you can find the matching pair,
They'll lead you through this forest fair."

To the BEACH

?

"But all these insects look different to me," said Fudge, trying to catch a large, blue dragonfly.

"And some of them don't look very friendly," muttered Blighty as a big bee buzzed past his ear.

"Well, we must look more carefully," said the Captain. And it wasn't long before Sinbad cried out, "Why, here they are. Quickly! Follow them before they disappear!"

Can you find two insects that are the same?

INTO THE JUNGLE

?

TO THE LAKE

D arkness had fallen by the time the mice
reached the island's sandy beach. It did not
take them long to set up camp for the night,
and soon Fudge had a fine insect stew simmering over
a fire. Sinbad struck up a jolly tune, and all the mice
joined in as he sang an old sea chantey. All, that is,
except for Horatio, who was busy looking at the
treasure map. As the last notes of the song faded into
the night air, he spoke up.

"We're being watched," he announced.

All the mice turned at once to look at the dark
forest that loomed a short distance from the beach.
And the more they looked, the more they fancied they
could see dozens of pairs of eyes shining at them out of
the darkness.

"The map says we will be watched through the night," said Horatio. "Then, in the morning, someone will come to fetch us."

"Someone ff...ffr...ffriendly?" stammered Blighty.

"Oh yes, I'm sure," said Horatio, trying to sound convincing. "But perhaps we'd better keep watch just in case."

So all through the night the mice took turns keeping watch on the eyes in the forest, until a cry from Flagpole Jo broke the early morning silence.

"Wake up everybody! Someone's coming!"

Match the eyes with the animals on the right to see who has just arrived to lead the mice across the island.

Eyes in the Night

Number 7, the woolly monkey, is the only one who did not watch the mice through the night. Did you notice that Nelson was watching them too?

1. Owl **2.** Umbrella bird **3.** Bush baby **4.** Spider
5. Gazelle **6.** Chimpanzee **7.** Woolly monkey
8. Leopard **9.** Macaque monkey **10.** Marten
11. Tamarin monkeys **12.** Boa constrictor **13.** Squirrels
14. Lizard **15.** Crested finch

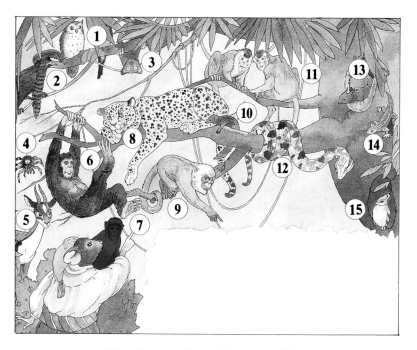

The Court of the Monkey King

Here is the only monkey who has nothing wrong with his clothes. You can see what is wrong with the others by looking at the list below. Did you also spot Nelson holding a gold coin in his beak?

1. Two halves of suit are different colors.
2. Trouser legs different lengths.
3. Trouser legs different colors.
4. Sleeves are different.
5. Odd shoes.
6. Odd pockets.
7. Button missing from jacket.
8. Collar is different either side.
9. Sleeves different lengths.
10. Decoration missing from one shoulder.
11. Odd socks.
12. One shoe missing.
13. Button missing from cuff.

X marks the spot

Here is the X. You should have found all the other letters of the alphabet as well. Did you also see Nelson hiding in the palm tree?

The Empty Chest

Have you guessed? It was Nelson who got to the treasure first. There he is, laughing at the mice from the top of the palm tree. He has scattered the treasure all over the island. Look back over the pictures and you should find all the things listed below.

Chalice; 2 Sapphire rings; Brooch; Sapphire bracelet; Fan; Ruby necklace; Pocket watch; String of pearls; Emerald ring; Ruby earrings; Diamond necklace; 14 Gold coins.

HAPPY HUNTING!